This book is dedicated to my amazing best friend and husband, Balan, our three little Indians, Vasan, Leela, Meera Asha, and all the children of the United States military because they serve, too!

www.mascotbooks.com

For more information, please contact:
Mascot Books
560 Herndon Parkway #120
Herndon, VA 20170
info@mascotbooks.com

Library of Congress Control Number: 2012955321

CPSIA Code: PRT0715C
ISBN-10: 1620862417
ISBN-13: 9781620822414

Printed in the United States

COUNTDOWN
'TIL DADDY COMES HOME

written by
Kristin Ayyar

illustrated by Melissa Bailey

My daddy is going on a trip.

I want to go with him, but I
can't fit in his suitcase.

I don't want Daddy to go!

But he says, "It's my duty to go.
Somebody else's daddy or mommy
would have to go if I didn't."

I wish nobody had to go. Then Daddy would be home to read me books and tuck me in every night.

Saying goodbye to Daddy is so hard! We cover his face with kisses and hug him tight. Daddy says that he'll see me in his dreams.

My daddy always comes back but waiting for him is hard. My mommy, sister, and I use a special chart to countdown the days 'til Daddy comes home.

During our countdown, Nana visits more and we plan cool things to make the time go by faster. It's fun, but I still miss Daddy.

Daddy can't call or talk to us on the computer every day when he's gone, so Mommy helps me write a list of things to tell him when we can talk.

Then I will remember to tell him about losing my first tooth and seeing real dinosaur bones at the museum.

This is my special treasure box.

Inside, I keep all the cool things I want to show Daddy when he comes home.

I have my tooth that the Tooth Fairy let me keep and things I find when Mommy takes my sister and me on adventures.

At bedtime, I really miss Daddy. That's when I hug my Daddy Bear and read books that have Daddy's voice in a magic box.

Before Mommy turns off the lights, she always gives me two goodnight kisses: one from her and one from Daddy.

Daddy sends us postcards and
letters during his trip. We always
look to see where he is on the globe.

Sometimes, he is really far away.

We send Daddy letters and care
packages filled with my drawings
and things he can't buy where he
is working. I wish I could fit in
the care package, too!

Sometimes, Daddy goes on really long trips. Our neighbor, Steve, comes over to our house and fixes things that Mommy can't.

Steve plays catch and wrestles with me like Daddy does. Mommy doesn't wrestle. She thinks wrestling is for sweaty boys.

The day before Daddy comes home is the longest day of all! Mommy makes Daddy's favorite foods and my sister and I help clean up the house.

We all make a big sign that says "Welcome home, Daddy!" I am so excited, I can hardly remember all the things I want to show and tell Daddy!

The countdown is over!
Daddy is coming home today!

My sister and I hold our "Welcome home" sign and wait for Daddy!

Daddy is finally home! Mommy makes sure we each get special time with him.

We spend our Daddy-and-son time wrestling and playing catch. I finally get to show him all the stuff in my treasure box, and he tells me all the things I would have seen if I could've fit in his suitcase.

Discussion Questions

Do you want to do anything special to say goodbye to Daddy?

Do you know why Daddy is going away?

What will you miss most about not having Daddy home? Can someone else do the things Daddy does while he's away?

Are you ever mad at Daddy for going away?

Do you know where Daddy is going and when he'll be back?

Where do you think Daddy will be living while he is gone?

Are you worried if Daddy will be safe?

How can we help you stay connected to Daddy while he is gone?

What type of comfort item should we get you? (Daddy bear or pillow case with Daddy's picture on it, etc.)

How should we countdown the days 'til Daddy comes home?

How should we break up the time so the countdown flies by?

How do you think we are going to be able to communicate with Daddy? How often?

Where do you want to keep the special things you want to show Daddy when he gets home?

If we send Daddy a care package, what should we put in it?

What can you do to help get ready for Daddy's arrival?

What should we cook for Daddy when he gets home?

What do you want to do for your Daddy-son or daughter time?

Four Ways to Countdown

Surprise Slips

Cut a slip of paper for each day or week the parent will be gone. Have family members write an activity on each slip of paper and place in a jar. Pull one out each day or week to enjoy a surprise activity. This does not have to cost a lot of money! It can be as simple as having a picnic at the park, family slumber party, or having ice cream for dinner.

Long Distance Kisses

When a parent is gone, one of the things kids miss most are hugs and kisses. Get a jar for each child and fill it with chocolates, one for each day the parent will be on the trip. Then, the parent who's leaving puts air kisses in the jar in front of the kids so the chocolate kisses are covered with real kisses. It's fun to see the jar slowly empty and get a sweet "kiss" each day from their parent.

Calendars

Create two personalized calendars to cross off each day the family will be separated. Fill your child's calendar with pictures of their parent and the parent's calendar with pictures of the family. Young children have a hard time with the concept of time and seeing it visually will help them understand the length of their parent's trip.

Paper Chain

There are two methods to use a paper chain for your countdown. The first is a countdown chain, where you make a paper chain with one link for each day the parent is going to be gone and remove one each night. The other way is a count-up chain where you add a link to the chain day by day, giving you a real perspective on how long a parent has been gone. It is also a great idea to write something about your day on each link creating a kind of journal. If you do the countdown chain, save the links in a jar or put on a scrapbook page to share them with your loved one when they get back.

Please visit www.daddycountdown.com to download a printable countdown chart or "Things to Tell Daddy" list and discover even more ways to countdown.

About the Author

Kristin Ayyar is the mother of three wonderful children, an avid volunteer in her community, and was an Air Force spouse for 27 years. *Countdown 'til Daddy Comes Home* is a book based on her family's experiences and is filled with rituals that she and her children follow when her husband is traveling the globe or was deployed overseas serving our nation.

Please visit **WWW.DADDYCOUNTDOWN.COM** for ideas on what you should do before you say goodbye, and explore ways to stay connected to ease the burden of your child's separation from a parent.

About the Illustrator

Melissa Bailey doesn't remember a time when she wasn't drawing. And she LOVES books. So pursuing a career illustrating children's books seemed a natural progression for this kid-at-heart. *Countdown 'til Daddy Comes Home* is her eighteenth children's book.

Past and present samples of her work can be seen on her website www.melissabaileyillustrates.com.

Please visit
WWW.DADDYCOUNTDOWN.COM
for ideas on what you should do before you
say goodbye, and explore ways to stay
connected to ease the burden of your
child's separation from a parent.

Acknowledgments

There are so many people who helped make this book possible. First, special thanks to my friends, family, and Melissa Bailey who all helped me refine my vision of this book and told me I could make it a reality. A big thank you to all my Kickstarter backers who believed in my project and invested in getting this book published. Thanks also to Amy Ester for the adorable dedication picture and my son, Vasan, who is my chief techie. I am truly grateful to everyone who helped me on my journey of becoming a published author. It is my sincerest hope that in sharing my family's traditions, this book will help young children cope with separations and help families stay connected.